Welcome to ALADDIN QUIX!

If you are looking for fast, fun-to-read stories with colorful characters, lots of kid-friendly humor, easy-to-follow action, entertaining story lines, and lively illustrations, then **ALADDIN QUIX** is for you!

But wait, there's more!

If you're also looking for stories with tables of contents; word lists; about-the-book questions; 64, 80, or 96 pages; short chapters; short paragraphs; and large fonts, then **ALADDIN QUIX** is *definitely* for you!

ALADDIN QUIX: The next step between ready to reads and longer, more challenging chapter books, for readers five to eight years old.

Buttons's Talent Show

Read the other books in the Pet Pals series!

PET PALS

Buttons's Talent Show

by ALLISON GUTKNECHT

illustrated by ANJA GROTE

Q QUIX

ALADDIN QUIX

New York London Toronto Sydney New Delhi

ALADDIN QUIX
Simon & Schuster Children's Publishing Division
1230 Avenue of the Americas, New York, New York 10020
First Aladdin QUIX paperback edition September 2022
Text copyright © 2022 by Allison Gutknecht
Illustrations copyright © 2022 by Anja Grote
Also available in an Aladdin QUIX hardcover edition.
All rights reserved, including the right of reproduction in whole or in part in any form.
ALADDIN and the related marks and colophon are trademarks of
Simon & Schuster, Inc.
For information about special discounts for bulk purchases, please contact
Simon & Schuster Special Sales at 1-866-506-1949
or business@simonandschuster.com.
The Simon & Schuster Speakers Bureau can bring authors to your live event. For more information or to book an event contact the Simon & Schuster Speakers Bureau at 1-866-248-3049 or visit our website at www.simonspeakers.com.
Series designed by Laura Lyn DiSiena
Cover designed by Alicia Mikles
Interior designed by Ginny Kemmerer
The illustrations for this book were rendered digitally.
The text of this book was set in Archer Medium.
Manufactured in the United States of America 0822 OFF
2 4 6 8 10 9 7 5 3 1
Library of Congress Control Number 2022931690
ISBN 9781534474055 (hc)
ISBN 9781534474048 (pbk)
ISBN 9781534474062 (ebook)

For Folly,

my loyal and loveliest light

Cast of Characters

Buttons (BUH-tens): Shy kitten at Whiskers Down the Lane Animal Shelter

Mitzy (MIT-zee): Excitable toy poodle at the shelter

Gus (GUS): Large guard dog at the shelter

Ted (TED): Manager of Whiskers Down the Lane Animal Shelter

Luna (LOO-nuh): Cranky cat at the shelter

Ruby (ROO-bee): Talkative woman who wants to adopt a cat

Contents

1

Tricks and Treats

"Hurry, Mitzy!" **Buttons** calls. "Ted will be here any second."

"One more time. Pretty please?" **Mitzy** begs the kitten. Her tongue hangs down the side of her curly white face, panting.

Buttons sighs. "Fine." He trots to where Mitzy's squeaky purple ball has rolled to a stop. After nudging it with his nose, he steps back. "Ready?"

"Yes, yes!" Mitzy scampers in place.

Buttons arranges his leg like a

golf club. "And…fetch!" He whacks the ball in Mitzy's direction.

"I got it!" Mitzy exclaims. She runs toward the ball, but her paws slip and she slides past it.

"Alert! Alert!" **Gus** barks with a frantic bounce. "Intruder approaching! I repeat, intruder approaching!"

"Oh no!" Buttons cries. "Mitzy, get into your cage!"

"Hold on. I need my ball," Mitzy insists.

"There's no time!" Buttons

protests, but Mitzy darts after the ball anyway. As the front door jingles with the sound of keys, Buttons dives into his own cage.

"Good morning!" **Ted**, the manager of Whiskers Down the Lane Animal Shelter, enters and then comes to a sudden halt. "Mitzy! What are you doing in the middle of the lobby?"

Mitzy answers with a huge **SQUEAK** from her ball before tossing it aside. "Buttons and I were playing fetch! Do you want to play with me now, Mr. Ted?"

"He's not looking for an invitation," **Luna** tells her, rubbing a paw over her whiskers. "He's asking how you **escaped**."

Ted crosses the room to examine the latch on Mitzy's cage. "The lock doesn't look damaged...."

"Did you bring any treats with you?" Mitzy asks, reaching up to scratch at Ted's pants pockets.

Ted brushes her away. "Sit, Mitzy. I'm trying to figure out how you broke free."

"And I am trying to figure out if you have treats," Mitzy says. When Ted kneels for a closer look, she hops onto his thighs.

"No!" Ted lowers Mitzy to the ground. "Sit!" he repeats, but she does not obey. Ted giggles under his breath. "It's a good thing you're cute, Mitzy, because you're not always the best listener." He scoops her up and places her in her kennel, then closes the clasp carefully. "Now, how did you figure out how to open this? That's the **mystery**."

He peers around the lobby, searching for an answer. Luna's round green eyes stare at him without blinking, revealing no secrets. Next to her, Gus is busy licking the metal grates like they're made of Popsicles.

"Hmmm. Maybe I didn't close it tightly last—" Ted stops himself when he spots something curious. Slowly he approaches Buttons and points at the kitten's tiny front foot, which is hanging outside his cage's door. "What's going on here?"

"What? Here?" Buttons mews nervously. "Nothing much."

Ted reaches a finger toward Buttons's paw and taps it with a quick "Boop!" Surprised, Buttons lets go of the door. **SCREECH.** It creaks open.

"So it was you!" Ted says. "I

didn't know you were so sneaky."

"Excuse me, Mr. Ted?" Mitzy pipes up from next door.

"Sit, Mitzy," Ted commands. "I'll be with you in a minute."

Mitzy remains standing, but Buttons plops onto his bottom.

Ted's eyebrows glide up his forehead. "Do *you* know how to sit?" he asks the kitten. "Let's try that again." He lifts Buttons to his feet and repeats, "Sit!"

Buttons does so instantly.

"Mr. Ted, excuse me," Mitzy

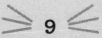

calls again, tap-dancing around her cage. "But you did not answer my question about the treats."

Ignoring Mitzy, Ted pats Buttons's small head. "I think we just figured out how to get you adopted. Let's see what other tricks you can learn!"

2

High-Five

Whenever Ted has a free moment during the day, he practices with Buttons. By evening Buttons can not only sit on command, but fetch, too!

"What do you think?" Ted

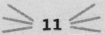

asks, digging into his pocket for snacks. "Should we try one more trick before closing?"

"How come Buttons is getting all the treats?" Mitzy whines. "I would like treats too."

"You don't know how to do anything," Luna points out.

"I do so!" Mitzy says, defending herself. "I can sit! I can come! I can fetch!"

"You *can*," Luna corrects her. "But you *don't*."

"Are you ready?" Ted settles

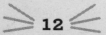

onto the floor with Buttons. "You're going to learn how to high-five." He turns his hand so his palm faces the ceiling. "Now . . . high-five!"

Buttons tilts his head and peers at him, **attempting** to understand what Ted wants him to do.

"High-five!" Ted encourages him. "High-five!"

Confused, Buttons lies down and crosses one leg over the other, hoping he got it right.

"No, high-five." Ted

slaps his own palms together.

"He wants you to jump onto his hand!" Gus says, coaching Buttons.

"I can do it!" Mitzy hurls herself against her door. "Buttons, let me out of here. I will show you what to do."

"Mitzy, stop that! You're going to hurt yourself." Ted leans over and releases Mitzy's lock so she can join them.

"High-five me!" Mitzy begs Ted, jumping over his arm and settling in his lap. "I would like

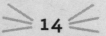

the treat. Give me the five!"

"If you want to stay out here with us, you need to be calm," Ted says, shifting Mitzy onto the floor. "Come on, Buttons. High-five!" He raises his hand as high as his shoulder, and out of nowhere, Mitzy takes a flying leap toward it.

"Whoa!" Ted catches her in midair. "Where do you think you're going?"

"I am high-fiving you," Mitzy explains. "Now give me the treat, please."

Ted holds Mitzy against his side and returns his attention to Buttons. "Let's try this again." He holds a treat in front of Buttons's nose so that he can sniff it. Then Ted moves it up. "High-five!"

"I did that already!" Mitzy squirms toward the food.

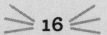

"He must want you to smack his hand," Luna tells Buttons. "It's the only thing that makes sense."

"Are you sure?" Buttons raises one paw **timidly** but then places it back on the ground.

"Give it a whirl," Luna says. "What's the worst thing that can happen?"

"The worst thing that can happen is that I do not get a treat!" Mitzy replies.

Buttons lifts his foot cautiously and extends it toward Ted's hand.

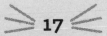

With a soft swipe he connects with Ted's palm.

"You did it!" Ted cheers. He places the treat next to Buttons and gives him a scratch under the chin. "You are amazing!"

Suddenly Gus's tail stands straight with alarm. "Alert! Alert!

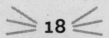

Intruder approaching!" he barks. "I repeat, intruder approaching!"

"Quiet down, Gus." Ted shushes him. "Maybe this is someone who's looking to adopt one of you. Buttons, you can show off your new tricks!" He carries Mitzy to her cage and then gazes around the room. "Buttons?"

The kitten is nowhere to be found.

As the front door opens, Mitzy calls out, "If Buttons is hiding, can I have his treat?"

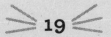

3

Fraidy-Cat

Later that night, Mitzy places her mouth around the rods of her cage, testing their strength. "Buttons, help me open this!" She bites down on a rung and tries to tear it.

"That's not how metal works,"

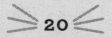

Luna says from across the dim room.

Mitzy chomps down harder. "I want to see if Mr. Ted dropped any treats before he left!"

"You're going to knock out all your teeth," Luna warns. "Treats aren't much good if you can't chew them."

"Maybe we should stay put tonight," Buttons says. He is camped out beneath his bed with just the tip of his tail sticking out.

"You know, the Bite Buster took

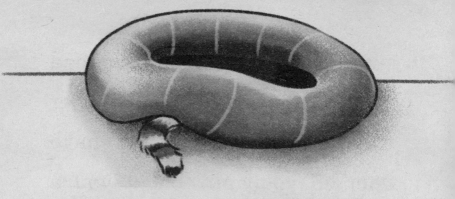

away your blanket so that you'd
stop hiding all the time," Luna
points out. "Not so you'd find a
new spot."

"It's cozy under here," Buttons
replies, defending himself.

"I miss being cozy," Gus says.
"None of the beds here are big
enough for me." He pushes unhap-
pily at the thin pillow beside him.

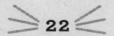

"If you hadn't barked your head off at the lady who came in earlier today, maybe she would have adopted you and bought you a bed," Luna tells him.

"She was interested in a cat, not a dog," Gus reminds her.

"Which is not very nice!" Mitzy adds.

"Buttons, you should have shown her your new tricks," Gus says. "Why didn't you?"

"I didn't feel like it," Buttons says stubbornly.

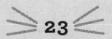

"You never feel like it," Luna tells him. "That's the problem."

Buttons crawls out from under his bed and perches at the front of his cage. "What does that mean?"

"Look," Luna begins, "you're not a bad-looking cat. You're smart, and you have a nice enough **personality**. But you don't believe in yourself. You don't think you're worthy of someone taking you home."

Buttons lowers his face and stares at his toes. "This is my home."

"For now," Luna says. "Not forever."

"But I'm comfortable here," Buttons protests.

"You're still very young," Luna says. "You deserve to know what a real home is like. Gus, Mitzy, and I—we've had that already."

"How is a real home different from here?" Buttons asks.

"Oh," Luna says softly, "in a million ways. There are windows to look out whenever you wish."

"And comfy sofas that are big enough to hold you," Gus adds.

Mitzy springs up. "And a person who is happy to see you!"

"You can always find a patch of sunlight," Luna explains. "Or a heating vent."

"And if you're really lucky," Gus says, coiling his tail around his body, "a fireplace."

"Plus, you know who you belong to," Mitzy agrees. "And who belongs to you."

Luna looks deep into Buttons's amber eyes. "That's what a real home is like. You haven't had one yet. And you never will if you spend your whole life being a fraidy-cat."

Buttons stays still for a moment and lets their words sink in. Then he turns toward his bed and shimmies underneath.

"So much for that," Gus scoffs.

But a second later Buttons slinks back into the open, Luna's toy mouse grasped in his mouth. He places it down and faces his friends.

"Okay," he says. "I am ready to be brave."

4

The Boss

Buttons and Luna sit on top of the lobby desk as Gus keeps watch out the front door.

"Here's what we're going to do," Luna announces. "The best way to gain **confidence** in your skills

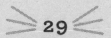

is to teach them to someone else. It's time for you to become a boss."

"*Your* boss?" Buttons asks.

"Don't be ridiculous," Luna says. "I'm my own boss, and Mitzy, well . . ." The two cats watch Mitzy, with her snout aimed at the ground, walk straight into a wall. "You know what they say about teaching old dogs new tricks."

Gus pulls himself up onto his rear legs to get a better view. "I can't see a thing! How am I supposed to perform my guard dog

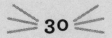

duties with no moonlight?"

Luna gives Buttons a sly look. "That's your student."

"Gus?" Buttons is shocked. "But he's so big!"

"So?" Luna responds. "What does size have to do with anything? Go ahead. Show him who's in charge."

"I don't know . . . ," Buttons says. "I feel bad telling him what to do."

"Think about it this way," Luna begins. "Gus loves rules. He likes following directions. You'd be doing him a favor."

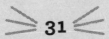

"Okay." Buttons takes a deep breath. "Here goes nothing." He jumps down and tiptoes to the door, then taps the end of Gus's bushy tail. "Um, Gus? Do you want to learn a trick?"

"It's not his choice!" Luna hisses. "Remember: you're the boss."

Buttons widens his stance to appear larger. "Gus, I am going to teach you how to high-five. Come with me."

"Yes, sir!" Gus turns around and follows Buttons across the room without question. "I am reporting for duty!"

"Where are you taking Gus?" Mitzy asks. She trots over to Luna and stares up at her friend. "Do you know where they are going?

Did they find treats somewhere?"

"The whole world doesn't revolve around treats," Luna tells her. "Now stop asking so many questions. You might learn something."

Luna and Mitzy watch as Buttons leads Gus to the far corner of the lobby. Then he faces the dog. "Okay, Gus," the kitten starts. "I'm going to hold out my paw . . ." Buttons reveals the small pads on the bottom of his foot. "And when I say, 'high-five,' you—"

SLAP!

Buttons darts out of the way just before Gus's gigantic paw hits the floor.

"Did I do it?" Gus asks hopefully.

"You almost squashed Buttons!" Mitzy yells at him. "You need to be more careful!"

Gus, **ashamed**, lowers his eyelids. "I am very sorry."

"No, no, it's fine," Buttons replies, comforting him. "We're still practicing. Remember to take it slowly, one step forward, one paw at a time." He raises his leg. "Ready . . . set . . ."

BAM!

Gus's paw swoops down as Buttons whizzes to safety.

"GUS!" Mitzy screeches.

"Oh dear," Gus cries. "Did I do it wrong again?"

"You're getting a little bit better," Buttons tells him kindly. "But wait for me to finish saying 'high-five,' okay?"

"Okay," Gus says. "I'll get it this time."

Once more Buttons lifts his paw and counts down, "Ready ... set ... high-five!" At the right moment Gus connects his foot with Buttons's as lightly as possible.

37

"You did it!" Buttons praises him. "Good dog!"

Mitzy scampers over. "Does Gus get a treat? If he does, can he please share it with me?"

"I don't have any treats," Buttons says. "But I do have an even better reward."

5

Soft Place to Land

Gus follows Buttons into Ted's dark office, and Mitzy jogs in behind them.

"Mr. Ted must keep treats in here," Mitzy says. She crawls under his chair until she reaches

the garbage can. "Ooh, trash! I love trash!" She spills a can full of ripped papers, used tissues, and an apple core.

Luna strolls into the room. "Put that down!" she yells at Mitzy, who is chewing on the sticky browned fruit. "Do you want to go to the vet because a stem is stuck inside your throat? Again?"

"But it is **delicious**," Mitzy insists.

While Luna argues with Mitzy, Buttons leaps onto a cabinet.

"Look what I found," he calls down.

Gus rises onto his rear legs and places his front feet against the top drawer. "Your blanket!" he exclaims. "I thought the Bite Buster took that away."

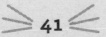

"I did too," Buttons tells him. "But I spotted it here when Ted was playing fetch with me."

"Shove it this way," Gus says. "I'll carry it to your bed for you."

"Actually," Buttons begins quietly, "I was wondering if you would like to have it."

"Me?" Gus asks. "You love that blanket."

"I do," Buttons says. "But I don't need it anymore. And it can help make your bed comfy. It's not a roomy sofa or a warm fire-

place, but it's still pretty cozy." He pushes the blanket with his head. "Take it."

Gus's lashes cover his eyes in one slow blink. "Are you sure?"

"I'm positive," Buttons insists.

He gives the blanket one last shove until it hangs just over the edge of the cabinet. Gus stretches his neck and opens his mouth. He grasps the wool between his teeth, then drags the blanket through Ted's office, across the lobby, and over to his cage. He drops it onto his thin pillow. Then he digs at the fabric like he's making a nest.

When he slumps down on top of it, the blanket is still only big enough to hold half of him, but for Gus it is more than enough.

Ted isn't alone when he arrives the next morning. The woman who visited the day before enters with him, and she is talking nonstop.

"I wanted to come before work to see the cat you showed me yesterday," she explains. "I thought I was interested in adopting a younger cat, but Oscar—his name is Oscar, right?—he was so handsome. But I'm not sure how he'll get along with my current cat, since they're the same age."

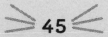

"Hi!" Mitzy hops up and down, trying to get the woman's attention. "I am Mitzy. Are you sure you do not like dogs?"

"Psssst, Buttons," Luna whispers. "This is your chance."

Buttons peeks out from beneath his bed, but he doesn't leave his hiding spot.

"Come on, Buttons!" Gus encourages the kitten. "Show this lady your skills."

Very slowly Buttons thrusts one paw out, followed by another.

 **46**

His ears appear next. Then his body slithers into view, and finally his tail. With Luna's toy mouse resting near his legs, he sits by his door.

"Hello," he mews in a shaky voice. "I am Buttons."

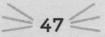

6

One Paw Forward

"Oooh, look at this cutie," the woman says, walking over to Buttons. "Hi there. I'm **Ruby**. What a sweet little kitty you are!"

"I am also **extremely adorable!**"

Mitzy pipes up from the cage next door.

"SHHHH!" Luna shushes her. "This isn't about you!"

Ruby pokes a finger through the grates to stroke the top of Buttons's head. Buttons grips the floor more tightly, forcing himself to stay put.

"That's Buttons," Ted says. "To tell you the truth, I've never seen him get so close to a stranger before. He must like you!"

"Then he has excellent taste!"

Ruby exclaims. "Can I see him out of his cage?"

"Of course," Ted agrees. "In fact, Buttons has learned a few tricks. Let's see if he'll do one for you."

Ted unlocks the latch and swings the door open. Buttons arches his back and pops out his claws, looking ready to flee.

"Don't you dare!" Luna yells.

"Show her how you high-five!" Gus says, cheering Buttons on. "Just like you taught me."

"You can do tricks?" Ruby coos, running her fingertips down Buttons's spine.

"He learned how to high-five yesterday," Ted says. "Do you want to show off, Buttons?" Ted holds his palm up in the air. "High-five!"

Buttons stays as still as a statue.

"Go ahead!" Gus prompts him. "Like we practiced."

"If you do it, you will get a treat!" Mitzy points out.

Buttons glances down at the toy mouse. Then he raises one leg, and with a fast swipe he slaps Ted's hand with his paw.

"Yes! Yes!" Gus barks.

"Hooray!" Mitzy exclaims. "Maybe you can share your treat with me?"

"WHEEEEEEEE!" Ruby squeals. She scoops Buttons up and cuddles him against her chest, covering him with kisses. "You are so talented!" She squeezes him with delight.

"No, NO, no, NO, no, NO!"
Buttons wiggles in her arms,
and frees himself from her grip
with a large twist. He leaps into
his cage and dives under his
bed, causing the whole thing to
shudder.

"Hmph.
I guess he
d o e s n ' t
like me as
much as I
thought,"
Ruby says

glumly. "Can we go see Oscar now?"

"Definitely," Ted agrees. "Let me grab the keys. You can feed him breakfast if you like." He closes Buttons into his cage and leads Ruby to his office.

"Mr. Ted did not give Buttons a treat even though he high-fived," Mitzy points out. "That is very unfair."

"I didn't want a treat." Buttons's **muffled** voice sounds from beneath his bed.

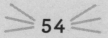

"Well, *I* would have eaten it!" Mitzy says.

"What happened?" Gus asks. "You were doing so well."

Buttons sticks out his head, like a turtle leaving its shell. "Ruby was loud. And she held me too tightly."

"That is because she thought you were cute!" Mitzy explains.

"I know," Buttons says quietly. "I messed up."

"I disagree," Luna tells him.

"You do?" Buttons asks with

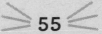

surprise. "But I was still a fraidy-cat."

"You did better than yesterday," Luna assures him. "That's something to be proud of. Plus, that lady was annoying."

"Why? I thought she was great!" Mitzy pipes up.

"Of course you did," Luna says. She focuses her gaze back on the kitten. "You'll know when it's the right person for you."

Buttons's whiskers twitch toward the ceiling until they

resemble a smile. "You really think so?"

"Of course you will," Gus agrees. "Like you said, one step forward, one paw at a time."

"Hey!" Ted calls from the next room. "Who dumped all this trash?"

The four pets look at one another in silence. Then Gus curls up on his blanket, Mitzy lies next to her squeaky purple ball, Buttons clutches his toy mouse, and Luna folds her front paws

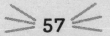

beneath her chest. Squeezing
their eyes closed, they pretend
to fall asleep, all braver together
than they are on their own.

Word List

adorable (uh•DOOR•uh•bull):
Really cute

ashamed (uh•SHAYMD):
Embarrassed about one's actions

attempting (uh•TEMP•ting):
Trying

confidence (KAHN•fuh•dents):
Belief in one's ability

delicious (dih•LIH•shuhs): Tasty

escaped (ih•SKAYPT): Got away

extremely (ihk•STREEM•lee):
Very

muffled (MUH•fulled): Having
the sound softened by padding

mystery (MIH•stuh•ree):
Something not understood

**personality
(PURR•suh•NA•luh•tee):** The
way someone usually behaves
and feels

timidly (TIH•mid•lee):
Nervously and shyly

Questions

1. How does Ted know that Buttons, rather than Mitzy, is the one who opened their cages?

2. Why does Buttons say he hides when strangers come into Whiskers Down the Lane?

3. What does Buttons give Gus as a reward?

4. Have you ever felt unsure of yourself? What do you do when you feel this way?

5. Are you more shy, like Buttons, or more outgoing, like Mitzy? Or are you a little bit of both?

6. What trick would you teach Buttons to perform?

QUIX FAST★FUN★READS

LOOKING FOR A FAST, FUN READ?
BE SURE TO MAKE IT ALADDIN QUIX!

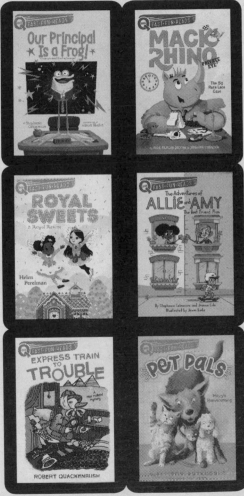